MODERN CHAOS!

by
MORT WALKER
and **DIK BROWNE**

TOR ®

A TOM DOHERTY ASSOCIATES BOOK
NEW YORK

HI AND LOIS: MODERN CHAOS

Copyright © 1983, 1989 by King Features Syndicate, Inc.

A TOR Book
Published by Tom Doherty Associates, Inc.
49 West 24 Street
New York, NY 10010

ISBN: 0-812-56928-8   Can. ISBN: 0-812-56929-6

First edition: March 1989

Printed in the United States of America

0 9 8 7 6 5 4 3 2 1

Other HI AND LOIS books
published by Tor Books

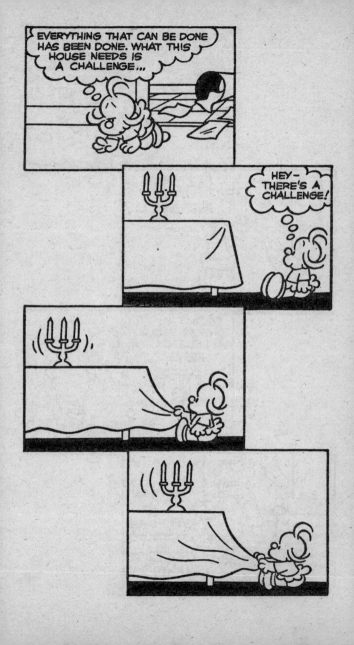

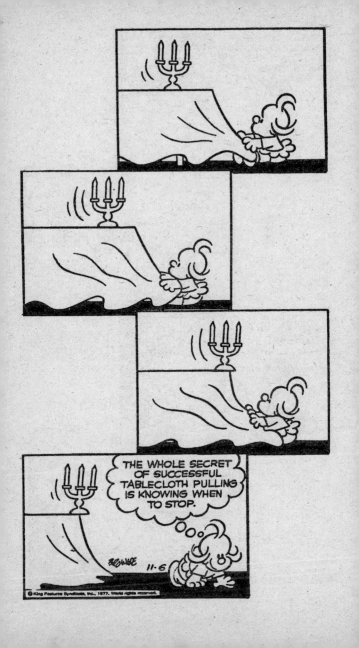

2-4

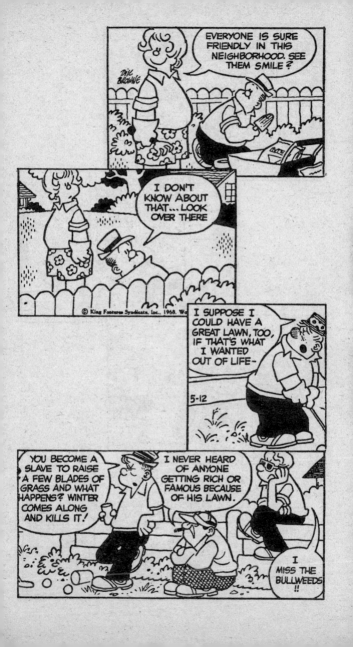

A TEMPERAMENTAL EXTENSION CORD
THAT WORKS ONLY IF YOU JIGGLE IT?

A
DOG DISH
THAT
SLIDES
?

A
SLIDING
DOOR
THAT
WON'T
?

A
CLOTHES ROD
THAT KEEPS
FALLING
DOWN?

FLAP FLAP

FLAP

A TRICKY
BEDROOM
SHADE ?

Congratulations!

YOU LIVE IN
A NORMAL
HOME!